CAPTAIN BLUEBOTTLE'S AMAZING TREASURE HUNT

CAPTAIN BLUEBOTTLE'S AMAZING TREASURE HUNT

Margaret Germon

For Lee

Contents   Page

CHAPTER 1

Mr. Bluebottle's Dream

It was just another long night at the Bluebottle house, on Seaview Lane.

Click, click, click went Mrs. Bluebottle's knitting needles, as she knitted a woolly winter scarf.

Roger, the green and red parrot, sat dreamily on his perch, by the window, as he tried to think of something interesting to say.

Mr. Bluebottle finished reading his newspaper, folded it neatly and picked up the television remote. Flick, flick, flick. He surfed through the channels, but he had seen it all before. With a sigh, he put down the remote and closed his eyes.

Tick, tock, tick, tock went the grandfather clock, in the corner of the room. Nothing else moved. It was as though time had finally stood still...

...Just another long night at the Bluebottle house.

Then a gentle breeze tugged at the net curtains, bringing a small puff of sea air into the quiet room. It wafted past Mr. Bluebottle. It tickled his nose and he breathed in deeply. It reminded him of seafaring days gone by, of adventures.

In his mind he saw tall ships, blue seas and sandy shores. He felt the excitement and he remembered the dangers. Golden treasure and stinking pirates! He felt the call of the sea.

Suddenly, he awoke with a bloodcurdling shout, that cut through the silence of the cozy room.

Mrs. Bluebottle dropped her knitting on the floor and looked at her husband with surprise. "Are you all right, Dear," she asked. "Did you have a bad dream?"

"Not a bad dream, Mrs. Bluebottle, a great dream!" said Mr. Bluebottle, as he leapt up from his chair. "I've had enough of watching the world go by. I've had enough of watching time pass, watching what I eat and watching my manners. I'm bored, Mrs. Bluebottle, totally bored! I haven't sailed a ship, sung a sea shanty or chased a pirate in years and I'm sick of it! I need an adventure and I need it now! I'm going back to sea!"

"Pirates!" squawked Roger. He flapped his wings and began to walk backwards and forwards along his perch. "Not the flaming pirates!"

"What a great idea, Dear!" said Mrs. Bluebottle. Her eyes sparkled, as she leapt up from her chair to hug Mr. Bluebottle with her biggest hug and to kiss him with her biggest kiss. "That's the best idea you've had for years. Things haven't been the same since you went normal. No swearing, no burping, no fun! So boring! Life has been a bit dull. And...no treasure! That's been the worst bit. I've really missed the treasure. When are you going, Dear?"

"Hmm, I could probably be ready to go by Friday, Mrs. Bluebottle. I'll write a list. Now, let's see...
I'll need..."
Ship
Captain's hat
Big black boots
Eye patch
Parrot
Captain's shirt and Captain's pants
Baked beans, bananas and bully beef
Rum
Fishing line
Fish hooks
Compass
Telescope
Crew

"Don't forget the treasure map, Dear," said Mrs. Bluebottle.

So, Mr. Bluebottle added...

Treasure Map

...and Mrs. Bluebottle added...
Toothbrush
Toothpaste
Soap
Clean Undies

"I think I'll take Ben with me," said Mr. Bluebottle. "He needs an adventure too. Kids these days don't often get the chance to have a rollicking good adventure."

"Are you sure?" asked Mrs. Bluebottle. "He's very young. I'm not sure he's ready for the tough sea life."

"Nonsense," said Mr. Bluebottle. "He'll love it. My Dad first took me to sea when I was ten and I had the time of my life. He showed me how to be a sailor, how to love the sea, how to find treasure and how to fight pirates. I've never forgotten that first adventure. It was the best time of my life. Shall we tell him now?"

"He's doing his homework," said Mrs. Bluebottle. "Let's not disturb him tonight. We can tell him in the morning at breakfast. He'll be so excited."

In the bedroom, next door, ten-year-old Ben Bluebottle sat hunched over his computer, as he feverishly played out his latest X Box adventure.

CHAPTER 2

I'd Rather be X Boxing

At breakfast the next morning, Ben Bluebottle could feel that something strange was going on. He noticed the looks that passed between his parents and it bothered him. Was he in trouble? He couldn't think of anything he'd done wrong lately.

His parents couldn't have heard about him being in trouble at school last week, for falling asleep during class. Surely not! After all, he had managed to convince the headmaster that his tiredness was caused by the stress and strain of too much homework. Hadn't he? He chewed his Cocoa Pops quietly and tried hard not to be noticed.

After a big silence, his father finished his bacon and eggs, put down his knife and fork and said, "Your mother and I have something important to talk to you about, Ben."

Ben wriggled in his chair. "Um, if it's about school, it wasn't my fault, Dad. It was too much homework."

"This isn't about homework, Son. This is about adventure. You probably don't know this, but some years ago, before you were born, I was a ship's captain," said his father. "I had my own ship and I sailed around the world for many years. I had adventures you would not believe. Lately I've been a bit bored with being just a bank manager, so I've decided to go back to sea and I'd like you to come with me. It will be a chance for us to have a real-life adventure together. What do you think?"

Ben looked at his father with amazement. He took in his neat grey suit, his polished shoes and his polite manner. His boring father...a sea captain! No way! He smiled at the thought. "Good joke, Dad. You're kidding, aren't you?" he said.

"Your Dad's not kidding, Ben," said his Mum. "For many years he was the bravest, most handsome captain, who sailed the seven seas. He survived terrible storms and difficult conditions in his search for buried treasure! He never gave up. He even rescued me from cruel pirates and captured my heart forever. When we were married, we decided that it was time for him to retire from the sea, to live a safer life on land, so he went to work at the bank."

Ben stared at his Mum, his not-very-exciting, ordinary Mum, in her cardigan, her floral dress and her fluffy slippers. He just couldn't picture her being rescued by anyone, particularly not by his even-more-ordinary Dad.

Still, his parents never lied to him, so it must be true.

He gulped. "Um, how long will we be away, Dad?" he asked.

"Let me think. Hmmm. We'll sail on Friday and be back in two months or so," said Mr. Bluebottle.

Ben frowned. The thought of spending two months, a month, a week, or even a day with his boring father didn't sound very exciting. "What would I do on board?" he asked.

"You'll be my Cabin Boy. It's a good job for a new sailor."

"That doesn't sound like much fun. What does a Cabin Boy do?" asked Ben.

"He does a bit of everything and he listens and learns so that maybe one day he'll be the Captain of his very own ship," said his father. "I started off as a Cabin Boy, you know."

"I'm sorry, but I really don't think I can go," said Ben. "I'll miss too much school and I'll get behind with my homework. You go, Dad, and I'll stay home and look after Mum."

"Nonsense," said his father. "I want you to come. Not all good learning comes from books, you know. I'll talk to your headmaster tomorrow. He'll understand..."

"Well, if you must know," interrupted Ben. He stood up from the table, his hands on his hips. "I really don't want to go. I want to stay here! On land! So, if you don't mind, I'm staying home. I've got some really important things to do."

"Things to do!" squawked Roger.

"You are coming," said Mr. Bluebottle firmly. "Your Mother and I have made up our minds. No arguing! You're going to love it, Ben. Now let's do some planning together."

"I'm not going, and you can't make me!" Ben stormed out of the room, with Roger close behind. He slammed the door. Soon the sound of loud music came through the wall.

"Oh, dear," said Mrs. Bluebottle. "That went down like a damp firework. He'll turn your adventure into a nightmare with his grumpiness. Maybe this isn't such a good time. Maybe we need to wait until he's a bit older. What do you think?"

"Nonsense," said Mr. Bluebottle. "He'll get over it."

But Ben, in the bedroom, wasn't getting over it. He sat on the end of his bed, deep in thought, planning how to get his own way.

"Adventure? You've got to be kidding me, Roger. It won't be an adventure. It'll be like a prison sentence. Just imagine spending two whole months stuck on a ship with my boring father! No way! Now, let me see...how can I get out of this?" He thought for a moment. "I know. I think a two-pronged attack will work.

"First I'll put on my sad face. That always works. After a day or two they'll start feeling sorry for me and Mum will be begging for me to stay home. And then if that doesn't work, at the very last minute, I'll get a ghastly disease. That should sort them out.

"Now don't disturb me, Roger. I'm about to have an adventure of my very own."

He turned on his X Box and settled in for the night

CHAPTER 3

Ben's Plan

For the rest of the week, the usually peaceful cottage on Seaview Lane was a hive of activity. There was a feeling of excitement in the air. There was so much to do in so little time.

Mr. and Mrs. Bluebottle worked hard to get everything ready and Ben worked hard to get his own way.

He put on his sad face and moped around the cottage for several days, looking for sympathy. But, unfortunately, no one noticed his unhappiness. His parents were just too busy.

By Thursday afternoon he realized that he would just have to work harder to make his plan work. At bedtime that night, he even managed to squeeze out a few tears. "I'm so upset, Daddy. I just don't think I'm old enough for too much adventure," he sobbed. "I want to stay home and work hard at school. Maybe I could go with you next time. Pleeease." He sniffed loudly and tried to look as upset as possible.

"Sorry, Son," said his father firmly, "Ten is the perfect age for a real adventure. I was just ten years old when I first went to sea. You'll be a great Cabin Boy.

Now get a good night's sleep. We've got a busy day ahead of us tomorrow." He kissed Ben on the top of his head, turned out the light and left the bedroom.

"Well, that didn't work," grumbled Ben. "I guess I'm going to have to get a disgusting disease after all. See how they like that! Bring me that red pen over there, Roger. I'll need some spots, I think."

In no time at all he had covered almost all his body with small round, red spots.

"You'll have to do my back and my bottom. I can't reach" he said, as he rolled over.

"Back and bottom!" squawked Roger, as he took the pen in his beak.

When Ben was satisfied that he was spotty enough he lay back, under the covers, eyes half-closed, with a pained expression on his face. "What do you think, Roger? Do I look sick enough?"

"Sick enough!" squawked Roger.

"Good," said Ben, as he hopped out of bed and turned on the X Box.

CHAPTER 4

Preparations and Disgusting Diseases

Eight o'clock came and went at the Bluebottle house the next morning. Mr. and Mrs. Bluebottle sat at the breakfast table, but there was no sign of Ben.

"Breakfast's ready, Ben," called his Mum.

No reply.

"Time to get up, Ben!" she called.

At that moment, a loud groan came from Ben's bedroom, followed by a strangled cry, "I feel so sick, Mummy. Sooooo sick."

Ben's parents looked at each other.

"Here we go. I wonder what he's got planned for us now." whispered Mrs. Bluebottle, as she headed towards Ben's bedroom.

"Are you ready, Dear?"

"Right behind you," whispered Mr. Bluebottle.

They opened the door

Ben lay on his bed, his eyes half closed, with a woeful expression on his face. He groaned and rubbed his stomach, "Ooh, ooh, I am so ill. Ooh, my head hurts, my stomach hurts! I know I've caught an awfully bad disease. I don't think I'd better get up today. Maybe I should have breakfast in bed, Mummy."

Mr. Bluebottle put his hand on Ben's forehead. "Will you look at those spots, Mrs. Bluebottle. That can only mean one thing."

"What's that, Dear?" she asked.

"This looks like a bad case of Cave Pox," said Mr. Bluebottle. "What do you think?"

Mrs. Bluebottle looked closely at her very spotty son, "You could be right. Oh dear, that's a worry. There's only one cure, you know." she said, in a very serious voice. "Let's hope we're not too late."

Ben managed to hide a grin. This was working out much better than he had expected.

"I'll feel better in a day or two, Mummy. I just need to stay in bed."

"Oh, no. Bed rest is the worst thing for Cave Pox," said his Mother. "I know of a boy who had Cave Pox. He stayed in bed and the next thing you know, his toes turned green and dropped off one by one. It was a terrible thing! He was never the same again.

"Fresh sea air and sunshine, that's the only cure. Come on, Ben, up you get. Cave Pox can turn nasty if it isn't treated straight away. We need to get you out of that bed and onto the ship as soon as possible."

With a groan, Ben crawled out of bed. He knew when he had been beaten.

CHAPTER 5

Setting Sail

That afternoon Ben stood alone on the deck of his father's ship, *The Breeze*, and looked around. He saw two tall masts, lots of rigging, sails, ropes, chains, a wheel, a captain's cabin and not much else. He began to wonder if it even had an engine. This ship was old! Really old!

"*The Breeze*," he muttered angrily to himself. "They should have called it *The Old Fart*!" The ship creaked. It sent a shiver down his spine.

From his vantage point, he looked down onto the pier and saw his father and mother below. His mother waved to him, but he didn't wave back. He was too angry. With a sigh, he turned away, picked up his bag and made his way below decks to find somewhere to hide.

Captain Bluebottle looked every bit a ship's captain in his new uniform, with its braided collar and shiny buttons. He adjusted his three-cornered hat, "Don't worry, Mrs. Bluebottle. He'll get over it," he said.

He gave his wife a big hug. "Are you sure you won't come with us?"

Mrs. Bluebottle smiled at her handsome husband. "Not this time, Dear. This needs to be a Father-Son

adventure. It's time for Ben to get to know wha
Dad is really like. Besides, I've too much work to uu
back here. We're having the annual beach clean-up
next month and it's my job to organize all the
volunteers."

"We'll get on our way now then, Mrs. Bluebottle.
We'll see you in about two months or so. Are you ready,
Roger?" asked Captain Bluebottle.

"Roger!" squawked Roger, as he sat on his
Captain's shoulder and looked very important.

"Adventure, here we come," said Captain
Bluebottle, as he strode up the gangway.

Mrs. Bluebottle waved goodbye. "Have a great
time, Dear," she called. "Have a great adventure and
bring back heaps of treasure. Give Ben my love when
you find him."

"I'll do that, Mrs. Bluebottle. We'll miss you,"
called Captain Bluebottle, from the bridge. He blew her
a big kiss and took his place at the wheel.

"We're ready to go, Crew," he shouted. "Haul up
the anchor, cast off the ropes, raise the sails and we'll
be on our way!"

Nothing happened.

"Where are you, Crew?" he shouted. "It's time to
haul up the anchor, cast off the ropes and raise the
sails!"

Still nothing happened!

"CREW! CREW! Where are you?"

He looked around. There was no sign of the crew.
He looked everywhere on the upper deck. No one in
sight! He looked in the lifeboats, he looked in the
galley, he looked in the mess and he looked in the hold.
No one in sight.

Finally, he looked in the bunk room below decks and there was the crew, all three of them, asleep in their bunks. Three lazy crew; one First Mate, one Cook and one Cabin Boy, all asleep, all snoring loudly.

"If I want anything done, I'll have to do it myself," grumbled Captain Bluebottle, as he returned to the upper deck.

"Give me a hand here, Roger," he said as he hauled up the anchor, set the sails and steered *The Breeze* away from the dock.

"Take care, Dear and don't forget to write," called Mrs. Bluebottle, as the ship sailed away.

All through that day and through the starry night *The Breeze* sailed on and on towards the treasure. All through that day and through the starry night, the three lazy crew snored on and on.

But not Captain Bluebottle and Roger. They were too busy to sleep.

"Yo, ho, ho
And a bottle of rum,
It's a Captain's life for me,"
sang the Captain, as he steered *The Breeze* past a pod of giant humpback whales.

"Do you know, Roger, that humpback whales are super special? They have two blowholes on the top of their heads. Most whales only have one."

"Yo, ho, ho,
And a bottle of rum,
I'm the Captain and I'm free!!!"
he sang as he sailed *The Breeze* past a school of playful porpoises.

"Here's a question for you, Roger. How can you tell the difference between a porpoise and a dolphin?"

"Squawk!" said Roger.

"No, it's nothing to do with their squawk, Roger. Do you give up?" asked Captain Bluebottle. "You look at their smiles, of course. Dolphins have longer lips. Porpoises have shorter, smaller grins."

"Treasure, treasure, here I come...
It will give me great pleasure,
To catch lots of treasure..."

sang Captain Bluebottle, as he steered through a flock of greedy seagulls.

"Did you know that seagulls have special glands above their eyes so that they can drink both freshwater and saltwater, Roger. Other birds don't have those. I guess that means that they don't get too thirsty when they are far out at sea."

"Squawk!" said Roger, from the tallest mast.

"Keep an eye out for pirates, Roger," called Captain Bluebottle.

"Pirates!" squawked Roger, with a shiver.

In the middle of the night, Captain Bluebottle paused for a moment to take his bearings from the moon and the stars and to check the treasure map. "Now, let me see. Here we are and there is Three Palm Island. If we keep sailing north-north-east, we should reach the island in about a month."

"Yo, ho, ho,
And a bottle of rum.
Buried Treasure,
Here I come!"

sang Captain Bluebottle, as he sailed *The Breeze* on and on through the starlit night.

Below decks, Brian, the First Mate, rolled over in his bunk and opened one eye. "Who's making all that noise?' he grumbled. 'It's not time to get up yet!"

"Is it breakfast time?" asked the Cook. He opened his eyes and rubbed his tummy.

"Are we there yet?" asked Ben, the Cabin Boy. "I'm bored."

"Quiet, Boy. Go back to sleep," ordered the First Mate. "Wake me for breakfast, Cookie."

The lazy crew went back to sleep, leaving Captain Bluebottle to do all the work.

CHAPTER 6

Fresh Fish for Breakfast

The next morning, at sun up, the lazy crew finally managed to drag themselves out of their bunks to the top deck. And, what an untidy-looking bunch they were! They looked quite disgusting. They looked like a band of grubby pirates and smelled like a bunch of stinky armpits.

They stood in an untidy line before Captain Bluebottle. "Attention, Men," he said. "Welcome aboard *The Breeze.* Welcome to a great adventure. I am Captain Bluebottle, the Captain of this ship. I expect hard work and high standards from you at all times. Is that understood?"

"Yeah, Man," said the First Mate. He eyed Ben and the Cook, with a nasty grin. "I'll make sure they work hard. You can rely on me, Man."

"You will start by addressing me as Captain or Sir," said Captain Bluebottle. He fixed the crew, with a steely look. "That means you too, Ben. Any questions, Men?"

"What's for breakfast, Captain? I'm starving!" said the Cook, as he burped loudly and rubbed his tummy.

"Breakfast!" squawked Roger, as he flew to the top of the tallest mast for some fresh air.

"I'm glad you asked that, Cookie. We're having fresh fish for breakfast this morning," said the Captain. "Is that okay with you?"

"Mmmmm, fresh fish," said the Cook. He licked his lips. "That sounds perfect. I quite fancy a bit of fresh fish and a cup of tea for breakfast."

"Well I don't want fish," grumbled Ben. He folded his arms and stamped his foot. "I want Cocoa Pops!"

"Cocoa Pops!" squawked Roger, the parrot.

"You'll have fish and like it," ordered the Cook. "Let us know when breakfast is ready, Captain. Until then, I think that I'll just have a little sit down and a rest in the sunshine. This sea air is wearing me out."

"Breakfast will be ready when you cook it, Cookie," said Captain Bluebottle. "Oh, and I'll have my fish lightly fried with a little tartare sauce on the side, please. Just let me know when it's ready."

Cook's eyebrows shot up and his mouth popped open. "Me...cook breakfast! I haven't had a very good sleep and now you want me to cook breakfast!"

"It's either that or we all starve, Cookie," said Captain Bluebottle. "Now be a good man and hop to it! I'm starting to feel hungry myself."

Cook stormed off to the galley, muttering and grumbling, like a wounded whale, only to return a few minutes later, muttering and grumbling even louder.

"Fish! Pish! How can I cook fish when there isn't any fish! Dah! What do you think I am? A flaming magician. No fish means no cook! So there!"

"There's plenty of fish, Cookie," said Captain Bluebottle. "First Mate just hasn't caught it yet.

"See that boat over there, Matey, that fishing line, those hooks and those worms. It's your job to catch the fish. I swear that my tummy is starting to rumble. One fish each should do it."

After a lot of grumbling, the First Mate rowed off in a real temper. He grumbled as he baited the hook with a fat worm. He swore as he cast his line into the water. He muttered under his breath, "I'll teach you not to boss me around, Bluebottle! Just you wait!"

A short while later, he felt a tug on the line. He gave it a little wiggle. There it was again. Another tug! Despite himself, he felt just a bit excited. "I've got a bite!" he yelled. "And it's a beauty!"

He whooped with excitement and jumped up and down with glee, as he reeled in his first fish. The small boat rocked precariously on the waves. "One down, three to go!" he called to the Captain.

"Sit down, Matey or you'll fall in," called Captain Bluebottle.

It took a while, but at last the First Mate had caught four fat fish.

"Fish! Pish! I'm not touching those smelly things!" grumbled the Cook. "They aren't ready to cook! Look! They have scales and tails, with slime and other disgusting stuff! Yuk! Keep those things away from me!"

"Fair enough, Cookie," said Captain Bluebottle. "The Cabin Boy will scale and clean the fish for you. Now, be a good boy and hop to it, Ben. I'm starving!"

"Me!!! Clean fish!! Not likely!" whined Ben. He wrinkled his nose and stamped his foot.

"Not likely," squawked Roger.

"It's either clean the fish or walk the plank," said Captain Bluebottle.

So, Ben cleaned the fish.

Cook cooked the fish.

They all ate the fish. It was delicious.

"Best fish I ever cooked," said Cookie.

"Best breakfast I ever ate," said Brian.

"Can we have fish for dinner?" asked Ben.

"Fish for dinner!" squawked Roger.

"BURP!!!" went Captain Bluebottle.

It was turning into a very good day.

CHAPTER 7

A Very Smelly Crew

"Now that we've finished breakfast, I'm just going to have a little lie down," said Cook, as he settled into a shady hammock. "Wake me up when it's time to cook tea, Captain. This life at sea is really starting to agree with me."

"Good idea, Cookie," said the First Mate. "I think I'll have forty winks myself. All that fishing has worn me out. That was the most work I have done in years. Wake me up when the sun is over the yard arm, Captain."

"Well, I'm bored," grumbled Ben. "There's nothing to do on this ship. No tv, no phone, no X Box...just nothing to do all day, except clean fish! I want to go home, and I want to go home now!" He folded his arms and looked angrily at his father.

"There's no time to sleep, no time to be bored, there's too much to do," said Captain Bluebottle.

"There are decks to scrub, dishes to clean, bunk beds to make. There are sails to furl, tales to tell and hornpipes to dance. On your feet, Men. Let's get to it!"

"Grumble, grumble groan," went the crew, as they filled buckets, scrubbed decks, washed dishes, made beds and cleaned up.

That is...two of the crew filled buckets, scrubbed decks, washed dishes, made beds and cleaned up. The First Mate pretended to work, but he really only gave orders.

"Tra, la, la!" sang Captain Bluebottle, as he steered across the deep blue ocean.

At last, when all the jobs were done, Captain Bluebottle and his crew sat down to a nice cup of tea. The ship sparkled from all their hard work.

"Time for a little rest for me," said Cook. "All this work has made me feel so.o.o.o sleepy."

"No time to rest yet, Cookie," said Captain Bluebottle. "You all stink a lot and I can't concentrate on sailing this ship with all that smell. So, it's bath time, Men."

The crew went below decks to have a bath. They had only been gone for a minute, when they came back, muttering and grumbling among themselves.

"Bath time, he says, but there is no bath," muttered the First Mate. "What do you think we are,

Captain? Flaming magicians or something! There is no bath and there is no shower. No bath means no scrub! So there!"

The smelly crew sat on their deck chairs and looked grumpy.

Captain Bluebottle smiled. "Calm down, Matey. There is a bath. You just haven't noticed it yet. Look over there. Yes, over there...past the railing... there it is... the biggest bath you will ever find. So, grab some soap and jump in...and, oh... don't forget to wash behind your ears."

Captain Bluebottle led the way. He stood at the railing and dived. With a giant belly flop, he splashed into the sea. "Last one in has to do the dishes tonight!" he called. He swam away, scrubbing as he went. "And that means you too, Roger!"

"No dishes!" squawked Roger, the parrot, as he too dived into the sea.

"We ain't doin' no dishes," shouted Cook, First Mate and Ben, as they raced each other to be first into the water. With teeth chattering, they swam after their Captain.

"Swim faster. You'll soon warm up," called Captain Bluebottle.

"What about sharks?" asked Cook. He looked around nervously.

"Swim faster so the sharks can't catch you," said Captain Bluebottle. He looked like a friendly dolphin, as he cut through the clear blue water.

So, they swam faster, and they soon warmed up. They swam faster, and the sharks stayed away. Around and around they went until they could go no further.

At last they pulled themselves back onto the deck and lay in a tired, sweet-smelling heap.

"Well done, Men," said Captain Bluebottle. "You've done so well! The ship is ship shape and you're starting to behave, look and smell, like a real crew should. It's time to rest now. It's been a good day."

"I think I'll just cook some dinner for us," said Cook. "All that exercise has made me hungry. Come on, Ben, do you want to help?"

"Sure thing," said Ben. "I'm starving! Do you want to help too, Brian?"

"Don't be ridiculous!" grumbled the First Mate. "I'm a First Mate, not a flaming kitchen boy."

"It's just that we need fresh fish for dinner," said Captain Bluebottle. "So, how about it, Matey?"

"!!!???***!!!" grumbled the First Mate.

CHAPTER 8

Seasickness and Lessons

Ben spent the next two weeks getting used to life aboard ship. It wasn't easy. He missed his home, he missed his Mum, but most of all he missed his computer games.

His days were filled with strange new experiences.

First, he had to get used to a rocking, rolling, ship. Up, down, up, down. It never seemed to stop. He felt that his head would never stop spinning and that his stomach would never stop heaving.

Captain Bluebottle said, "Just take it quietly, Ben, you'll feel better soon."

"Leave me alone!" shouted Ben. "You made me come on your stupid adventure, so now you can just leave me alone!" He stormed off.

It didn't help that the ship rocked at that very moment, causing him to lose his balance and his dignity, as he tripped over his feet and landed on his bottom.

"And now, look what you made me do!" he cried as he pulled himself upright and limped below.

The next morning, when Ben woke, he was surprised to find that he felt a lot better. The rocking didn't worry him any longer and he felt quite hungry.

He made his way down to the galley. "What's for breakfast, Cookie? I'm starving," he asked.

"Well, it's fresh fish again," said Cookie. "But we'll need to wait until Brian gets up, to catch the fish."

"Hmmm," said Ben, as he left the galley, in search of the Captain.

"Hey, Captain," he called as he reached the bridge. "We need fish for breakfast. I'm hungry and Brian's not up yet, so I've decided to do the fishing today."

"I'm not sure, Ben," said Captain Bluebottle. "Are you sure you're up to this? You were so sick yesterday."

"Well, I'm all right now," said Ben. He pulled on a lifejacket and lifted the fishing tackle into the rowboat. "Can you give me a hand to get this boat into the water, please?"

"If you promise not to go too far from the ship, I guess that's okay," said Captain Bluebottle, as he helped winch the boat over the side.

"I promise," Ben called. He lowered himself into the boat and tried to row away.

He soon discovered that rowing wasn't really that

easy. One oar always seemed to be stronger than the other. This meant that he spent the first few minutes rowing around and around in a circle, not going anywhere. Embarrassed, he concentrated on moving both oars in and out of the water together. His shoulders ached and a couple of times he nearly lost an oar in the choppy water, but he didn't give up and at last he managed to row in a straight line. He anchored a short distance from *The Breeze*, ready to do some serious fishing.

He baited his hook, tied the line to his big toe, threw it overboard and settled down to wait for the fish to arrive. He waited. And waited. Nothing happened. He closed his eyes and wished that he was back at home.

He was right in the middle of a wonderful daydream, when there was a huge tug on his toe. Ouch! That hurt! Another tug! He looked down into the water but couldn't see anything.

Very, very carefully, he untied the line from his toe, leaned back and started to reel in his catch.

That's when the fight began. Ben would pull, then something underneath the water would pull. It was a tug of war, which seemed to go on and on for ever. He felt like his arms were being pulled out of their sockets.

He kept fighting, reeling in a little at a time until he finally began to win the battle. At last, a huge, tired fish reached the surface and Ben was able to tow it back to the ship.

It took all his strength to pull the fish on board.

"Great catch, Ben," said Captain Bluebottle.

Ben ignored his father as he headed for the galley, with the giant fish over his shoulder. "Fish for breakfast, Cookie," he proudly announced, as he flopped the fish onto the bench.

"Great work, Ben," said Cookie. He reached for the fry pan. "This one's big enough for everyone."

At breakfast time, Ben announced, "I've decided to do all the fishing on this voyage."

"What do you think about that, Brian?" asked Captain Bluebottle.

Bleary-eyed Brian, who had just woken up, stopped mid-chew and frowned, "He's just a boy. What does he know about fishing? Next thing you know, he'll get into trouble and sink the jolly rowboat. Then where will we be?"

"Well, I've decided to give him a chance," said Captain Bluebottle firmly. "You go for it, Ben, I think you'll do a great job."

"Me too," said Cookie. "You did an awesome job of catching and cleaning our breakfast this morning, Ben."

"I won't let you down, Cookie," said Ben.

From then on Ben fished every day, sometimes twice a day, in all sorts of weather. He grew to love the hours spent alone in the little boat. Most of all he enjoyed the time away from bossy Brian.

Sometimes Roger would join him, and they would have long conversations that would go something like this…

"Don't look now, Roger, but there goes Brian, trying hard to pretend that he's being busy. He's just so lazy."

"Lazy!"

"You're right, Roger. Lazy and as grumpy as an old hippopotamus."

"Potamus,"

"I reckon if he smiled, his lips would take off with fright,

Roger.

What do you think?"

"Squawk! Squawk! Squawk!"

The two of them would roll around in the rowboat giggling.

One morning, after fishing, Captain Bluebottle announced, "We'll start your lessons today, Ben. Come up on deck after breakfast and we'll get started."

Ben looked at him with dismay. "I'd love to, but I don't have any books."

"Who needs books, when you have the ocean?" asked his father. "Just bring yourself and don't be late."

Ben stamped his foot. "Now you want me to do flaming lessons! It's not bad enough that you bring me on a boring adventure, now you want me to do boring lessons. It's not fair!"

"Not fair!" parroted Roger.

"See you on the deck," said Captain Bluebottle.

Up on deck, after breakfast, Ben stood, with his arms crossed and glared at his father. "I'm here, so where are the lessons? What are you going to teach me today, Captain?"

"I'm going to teach you how to tell the time by the sun, how to steer by the stars, how to work out how far you have travelled each day. I'm going to show you how to gather water, how to fill the sails with wind and how the tides work. You'll learn how to tie real sailors' knots and how to climb the tallest mast to the crow's nest," said the Captain. "And if you do well, one day I may even let you steer the ship. How does that sound, Ben?"

Ben's mouth popped open and, although he tried hard to stop it, a big smile took over his face. "Well, um, er, I guess that's all right," he said. "When do we start?"

"Right now, of course," said Captain Bluebottle.

From that day on, Ben looked forward to his learning, quite forgetting that he really didn't like lessons at all. He even started to like life on board and soon forgot to be angry with his father. He enjoyed the days, but most of all he loved the starlit nights, when the world seemed to become a magical place. There were stars to find and courses to plot, but most of all there were the stories... of pirates, of treasure, of adventure.

Ben was fast becoming a sailor in every way. He worked hard at his lessons and soon there was only one challenge left...the hardest of them all...the climb to the crow's nest. Each morning he would stand by the tallest mast and look up and up and up, until his neck would hurt. Most times he could see it, way, way up in the sky, perched at the top of the mast, but on a bad day it would be hidden by clouds. The only way up was by a fragile rope ladder, which would swing in the lightest breeze. The very thought of climbing that ladder made him feel sick.

Apart from that, his life on board was great...except for one thing... lazy Brian. Lazy, bossy Brian, who expected Ben to do all his work for him.

He seemed to take pleasure in making him feel small.

At first Ben tried his hardest, but nothing seemed to please the grumpy First Mate.

Then Ben tried to hide from him, but Brian would always find him. It was as though he had built-in Ben-seeking radar.

He was a big problem.

CHAPTER 9

What's Brian Up To?

It was near the end of another busy day at sea, when Ben cautiously uncurled his body from the floor of the rowboat, stored above the deck. He rubbed his aching shoulders and took a quick look around. No one in sight. He could just hear the men below decks. They were taking a break, after a hard day's work. He wanted to join them, but he stayed where he was. He was in hiding. He knew that if he was found Brian would give him even more work to do. And he had already done more than his share.

Lately it had been, "Do this, Boy. Do that, Boy. That's not good enough! Do it again, Boy!"

Nonstop!

He was already doing most of the First Mate's chores. He felt all used up and worn out.

As he settled back down into the boat for a nap, a small movement caught his eye. It was Brian, the First

Mate, coming up from below deck.

Ben held his breath and wriggled down onto the floor of the lifeboat. The sound of soft footsteps came closer and closer and then faded away into the distance.

Whew! That was close! Ben breathed a sigh of relief and lifted his head above the side of the boat, to watch the First Mate. He seemed to be acting strangely. He moved like an eel, slithering quietly along, pausing here and there for a moment to look around and to listen, before moving on again.

"I wonder what he's up to," Ben whispered to himself. "He's looking for something and it'd better not be me. I think he's up to no good."

He watched as Brian reached the Captain's cabin, tried the door and then disappeared inside, only to reappear several minutes later. He didn't look happy.

Ben shrank back down into the boat. He could hear heavy footsteps coming back towards him. He held his breath and crossed his fingers.

The footsteps went past.

Ben lifted himself for another look, but in doing so, he banged his knee on the side of the boat. It was a small sound, but it seemed to fill the air. He closed his eyes and tried to make himself as small as possible.

The footsteps stopped and then came back.

"Well, well, well. If it isn't little Ben, the lazy Cabin Boy," said a nasty voice. "I've been looking for you everywhere. There's work to be done and here you are just lounging around, doing nothing."

Ben opened his eyes and looked up. The First Mate loomed over him. He was so close that Ben could see the hairs in his nostrils quivering and could smell the remains of his last fishy meal on his breath. His stomach churned.

He scrambled out of the rowboat and stood up, his knees shaking. With a brave face, he stood tall and defiant.

"Just taking a small break, Brian. I wanted to be

fresh for my duties. What would you like me to do now?"

He looked the First Mate right in the eye. "Catch a whale? Fillet a sardine? Or perhaps I could even clean your boots for you. After all I seem to have done everything else."

Brian's mouth popped open as he grabbed at Ben. He caught him by the scruff of the neck and swung him into the air. "You want boots! You'll get my boot on your bottom! You want duties! I'll give you double duties!" he roared. "You'll be so tired, you'll be begging me to stop! I'll show you who's in charge here! Just you wait."

At that moment Roger flew down, with a loud, "Squawk". He divebombed the First Mate and distracted him for just a moment.

Ben managed to wriggle free and he dropped to the deck. He picked himself up and took off. He ran as fast as he could towards the bridge, with Brian following close behind.

"Just you wait till I get my hands on you!" shouted Brian, as he grabbed at him.

Ben didn't stop to listen. He just kept running. He could hear the First Mate coming after on him, so he took a short cut through the galley. "Hide me, Cookie!" he gasped, as he dived under the bench.

Just in time!

A moment later, Brian ran into the room. "Where did that boy go, Cookie?" he asked. "He's around here somewhere. I saw him come in. He can't be far away." He started to look around.

"He went that way," said Cookie. He shielded Ben from sight with his apron and pointed to the storeroom.

Brian shot into the storeroom and Cookie whispered to Ben, "Go, now! He'll be back any minute."

"Thanks, Cookie," whispered Ben, as he ran out the door, heading for safety. Behind him, he heard a loud shout, as Brian realised that he had been tricked.

Ben ran on until, at last, he could see his father on the bridge. He slowed to a walk and tried to look nonchalant. "Excuse me, Captain," he said. "Do you need any help with anything? I could tidy those ropes, if you like."

"Thank you, Ben," said Captain Bluebottle, with a smile. "That would be a great help."

"What do you think, Matey?" asked the Captain, as he turned to Brian, who was just arriving, puffing and panting heavily. "Ben's turning into a real sailor, don't you think?"

Brian growled under his breath.

"What was that, Matey?" asked the Captain. "You're looking a little tired. Maybe you need to do some extra exercises each day to help you get fit. What do you think?"

"Grrrr!" said Brian.

"Good man," said Captain Bluebottle. "We'll start in the morning. We'll have you fighting fit in no time. Now, let's go down to dinner."

The Captain and Brian left the bridge and headed for the galley.

Deep in thought, Ben stayed behind to tidy the ropes.

Captain Bluebottle called back over his shoulder, "You too, Ben. Just leave the ropes. You can finish those later. We're halfway to our destination and I have a very important announcement to make."

"Coming, Captain," called Ben, still deep in thought.

What was Brian doing in the Captain's cabin?

CHAPTER 10

An Extraordinary Adventure!

Dinner that night started out badly for Ben. He tried very hard to act normally, but he could feel the First Mate glaring at him throughout the meal. Ben kept his eyes on his plate and didn't speak.

"Are you all right, Ben? You're very quiet tonight and you've hardly touched your dinner." Captain Bluebottle's voice interrupted his thoughts.

"Yes, Sir, I'm fine," answered Ben, with a start. "I'm not really that hungry, Sir. May I please be excused? I think I might have an early night."

"Just a minute, Ben," said Captain Bluebottle, "I have some important news for you all. Roger, can you get the paper roll from its hiding place, please."

Ben watched, as the First Mate took a sudden interest.

"Hiding place!" squawked Roger as he flew out of the cabin, only to return a few minutes later, holding what looked like some sort of rolled-up scroll in his beak.

"Good Bird," said the Captain. He carefully unrolled the paper and laid it on the table, smoothing down the edges, to reveal a map.

"That looks like a treasure map, Captain," said the First Mate.

"You're right, Brian," said Captain Bluebottle. "It is a treasure map." He smiled. "You may have thought that we were out here for just an ordinary adventure, but that's definitely not the case. We're about to have an extraordinary adventure. We're on a hunt for buried treasure!"

"Buried treasure!" squawked Roger.

"Buried treasure," gasped the Crew, as they edged closer to see better.

"Yes," said Captain Bluebottle. He pointed to a spot on the map. "Look here. This is where we are now, and this is where we're going. See this island...Three Palm Island...that's where we're heading.

"If we keep going at our current speed, we should get there in about two weeks' time. We'll anchor offshore, we'll follow the map to the buried treasure, we'll dig it up and then we'll sail home. There'll be plenty of treasure for everyone to share."

"Wow!" said Ben. "Buried treasure! I can't wait!"

"Not so fast, Ben," said Captain Bluebottle. "Nothing good comes easy, I'm afraid. I'm telling you all about it now, because we're heading into very dangerous waters. This is pirate territory, the most terrifying corner of the seven seas. There are fierce pirates out there somewhere, sitting quietly, just waiting to catch us. They can sneak up on us at any time, so we need to stay out of their way and be ready to change course at a moment's notice.

"Roger, I want you to keep watch from the crow's nest each day. If you see a sail in the distance, call out and we'll change course immediately. It's really important that we see them before they see us."

"Aye, aye, Captain!" squawked Roger.

"From tomorrow, we're also all going to get up an hour earlier each day. We need to be ready for anything those beastly pirates might throw at us. Any questions, Men?"

"No, Sir!" chorused the excited crew.

CHAPTER 11

Letters Home

For the next two days there was a feeling of great excitement in the air. Even lazy Brian seemed to find some new energy and a better mood. Every morning there was ship cleaning and crew cleaning, every afternoon there was pirate training and every evening there was star watching, knot tying, story-telling, singing and dancing.

Roger spent many peaceful hours each day, high in the crow's nest watching for pirate ships, but saw nothing.

"Today is letter writing day," announced Captain Bluebottle one morning, as he handed out pens and paper to the crew. "It's time we wrote to our families."

Cook wrote:

Dear Sis,

I'm having a good time and am cooking lots and lots of fish for breakfast, lunch and dinner. Yesterday I got a bit tired of cooking fish, so I decided to cook a cake instead. But there were weevils in the flour!! Yuk!

But then Captain Bluebottle said why don't we have fried weevils instead. So, I fried up the weevils in batter and they tasted great! Just like crunchy peanut butter! Captain said that they were the best weevils he had ever eaten. I felt so proud!

Guess what! I might come back a rich man. The Captain told us that we are on a treasure hunt for real buried treasure! He's even got a treasure map! He says that there'll be enough treasure for all of us.

I'll try to bring you back a gold crown, Sis. And maybe some jewels. There might even be enough left over for me to have my own fish and chip shop, when we get back to land.

Wish us luck,
Your big brother,
Gregory

Ben, the Cabin Boy, wrote:

Dear Mum,

I miss you a lot! Dad's acting like a real ship's captain. He makes us all call him Captain Bluebottle or Sir. He doesn't even answer if I call him, Dad. I asked him why and he said that it's character building, whatever that means! He's a pretty good Captain, though and knows heaps about everything.

I was bored, but I'm not now so much, because ~~Dad~~ Captain Bluebottle lets me do lots of interesting stuff. If I work hard at my lessons, I might even get to steer the ship one day. We work all day, but the nights are pretty good. We get to tie knots, tell stories, sing songs and dance hornpipes.

Our trip is starting to get very exciting. I've just found out that we are looking for buried treasure and that we might meet up with mean pirates. I can't wait! Roger's keeping a lookout for pirates from the crow's nest, so we can see them before they see us.

Cookie is a lot of fun, but I don't like Brian, the First Mate, at all. He's so bossy! He's lazy and makes me do all his jobs. I think he's up to no good. I saw him sneak into the Captain's cabin the other day. He looked like he was looking for something.

Yesterday, when I was swimming, a huge shark came past and he looked like he wanted to have me for dinner. 'You're not going to get me, Sharkie,' I said. I swam round and around the ship, getting faster and faster. He couldn't keep up. Soon he got tired and swam away. Poor shark, he looked worn out!

We had fried weevils for dinner last night. Wow! These are even better than Cocoa Pops. I went back for seconds!

Your loving son,
Ben xxxxx

ps: Roger sends you a big 'Squawk'.

Captain Bluebottle wrote:

Dear Mrs Bluebottle,

I hope you are well. I'm having the time of my life.

When we started out, I thought that I had the laziest crew in the world, but they are slowly getting better. Ben is doing a great job as Cabin Boy and I think he's secretly enjoying himself. I am so proud of him. Even the parrot is working hard as a watch bird.

We'll probably get to Three Palm Island in a couple of weeks...that is if the weather stays good. I'm hoping to get lots and lots of treasure for you.

Cookie made fried weevils for dinner last night. Golly, gosh! I had forgotten how good those things tasted. They made my skin crawl with happiness! Yum!

We're sailing through dangerous pirate territory now, but so far, we haven't seen any pirates. If they come, I hope that we see them before they see us.

I'll write again soon.

Your loving husband,
Captain Bluebottle

The First Mate wrote:

Hi Bro,

Well, we're on our way to the treasure and that idiot, Captain Bluebottle, doesn't have a clue. He thinks I'm a First Mate, for goodness sake! He doesn't know that I'm the brother of Captain Marmaduke Mustard, the meanest pirate on the Seven Seas.

He let me have a look at the treasure map the other night and I now know that we're headed to Three Palm

Island. That's where the treasure is. We'll get there in about two weeks' time. I'll meet you there. I can't wait to see you.

Meanwhile I'll keep pretending that I'm a good First Mate. It's enough to make me want to throw up!

I've had enough of this ship, this Captain and his unbearable Cabin Boy son. It's clean this, clean that. Do this, do that. All day long every day! I'm a pirate not a flaming cleaner! And I'm sick of smelling like a flaming rosebud!

See you in a couple of weeks,

Brian

When they were finished, the crew put their letters into bottles, popped on the corks and posted them over the rail into the sea. They watched as they bobbed away into the distance.

CHAPTER 12

The Best Storm

For the next week *The Breeze* sailed peacefully on and on towards Three Palm Island and the treasure. The crew all worked hard, trained hard and the ship sparkled. There was no sign of pirates, so they all started to relax, just a little. Brian's mood even seemed to improve each day, which made Ben feel a whole lot safer.

"This is the life for me," said Captain Bluebottle, after a busy, sunny day and after a particularly large dinner of fish fingers and chips.

"I must say, Cookie, those fish fingers were divine. I'd have seconds, but I think I'll just turn in now. There's a feel of a storm in the air. Can you feel it, Men? I reckon we're in for a bit of a blow.

Matey, you take the first watch and then wake me at ten. Cookie and Ben, make sure that you get an early night. We have a big day ahead of us tomorrow."

"Aye, aye, Captain," said the First Mate. He sprung to attention.

"What storm?" asked Cookie. He stood and looked out to sea. It was a beautiful night. "There's no wind and the stars are shining. I'm not a child, Captain! I'll go to bed when I'm ready and not before! And I'm not ready yet!"

With that he sat down, plunk, in the biggest deck chair, with his arms folded and his moustache twitching.

"I'm not ready to go to bed yet either, Captain!" Ben stamped his foot and looked very disobedient. "I'm going to sit right here with Cookie until I decide it's time to go to bed."

He sat down right next to Cookie and waited for his father to say something. But Captain Bluebottle had already gone to his cabin and wasn't around to see the bad behavior.

"That's the way, Men," said Brian, "The Captain's dreaming. It's a beautiful night. There's not a cloud in sight. Feel like a game of cards, Cookie?"

"Don't mind if I do," said Cookie.

"Ben, you come up to the bridge and steer while Cookie and I play," said Brian.

"Me! Steer the ship! Wow!" shouted Ben. "Do you mean it?"

"Of course, I mean it," said the First Mate. "I said it, didn't I?"

"Um, I'm not sure how to steer a ship," said Ben, nervously. "How do I do it?"

"It's easy. Just hold the wheel, point the ship towards that star over there and don't let go. There's nothing to it. Now, don't disturb us. Cookie and I have some cards to play."

Ben nervously took the wheel. He crossed his fingers, pointed the ship towards the bright star and held on tight. *The Breeze* sailed on happily across the peaceful ocean.

It was easy at first, but then Ben noticed a light

breeze, then a fresh wind. "I'm finding it a bit hard to steer, Brian," he called. "The wind seems to be getting up."

"Do be quiet, Ben," shouted the First Mate, as he dealt another hand. "I can't think straight when you call out. Just hold on tight and you'll be fine. Do I have to do everything for you?"

Ben steered on through the dark, windy night. He held tight to the heaving wheel, as he struggled to stay upright. The wind became wilder and wilder and it was much harder to steer. His arms got very tired and he began to feel just a little afraid.

Flash!! A sheet of jagged lightning lit the sky. Boom!!!! A crash of thunder filled the air. The storm swept in with a wild tempest.

The ship's wheel turned sharply by itself, almost wrenching Ben's arms from his body. He could hardly hold on. He was terrified.

The game of cards finished abruptly. A strong gust blew the playing cards into the air, to be swept away into the darkness. The sky blackened, and the wild wind whistled.

And then the rain came. It bucketed down. The sails twisted inside-out and the deck became an angry torrent.

Brian and Cookie clung to the mast and looked very afraid.

Ben clung to the wheel.

"Get Captain Bluebottle!" shouted Ben. "I can't hold on any longer! I'm going to crash this ship! Help, Captain! Help! I can't hold on!"

In his cabin, Captain Bluebottle was awakened from a deep sleep, by a feeling that things were not going well.

"What was that sound, Roger? What's going on? Oh goodness me, things are bumpy in here, I'd better go and have a look. Hold on to me Roger, we can go together." He began to drag himself through the cabin door.

Roger held on tight with his eyes shut.

"It's the storm, Roger," said Captain Bluebottle. "Watch out for flying debris!"

"Squawk!" said Roger, as a bucket flew past, narrowly missing him.

"Whew, that was close," said the Captain, as he ducked out of the way of a swinging sail.

At last they managed to reach the bridge, just as a huge wave broke over the deck. *The Breeze* rolled violently, sending the Cook and First Mate flying by in an untidy tangle of arms and legs.

"Help, Captain, save us!" they shouted, as they skidded across the deck on their bottoms, heading for the side rails.

"Help, Captain, save us!" they shouted, as the ship rolled again, and they skidded past again, in the opposite direction.

Meanwhile Ben stood strong. He clung to the wheel, fighting the storm and just managing to hold on. "Help, Captain," he called. "I can't hold on much longer; this storm is too strong for me. Please help!"

"I've got it now, Ben," said Captain Bluebottle, as he took his place at the wheel. "Here, take this rope and tie it around your waist. Tie the other end to the main mast there. That way, you'll be safe.

"When I've steadied *The Breeze*, I want you to take two more ropes to Cookie and Matey, so they can be safe too. Yes, that's the way. Do stop grumbling, you two...it's only a storm. Now I need you all to help sail this ship."

But Cookie and Matey weren't having any of that.

"What do you mean, It's only a flaming storm?" grumbled Cookie. "I'm a cook. I don't do storms, Captain. I'm going to bed right now, so there! Call me when it's all over."

"Me too," snorted the First Mate, as he struggled to his feet. He rubbed his bottom. "Wake me when the sun comes out, Captain. I'm exhausted. Are you coming, Ben?"

"I'll stay and help the Captain," said Ben bravely.

"Thanks, Ben. I need you to get the sails down, before the ship keels over. It's not an easy job for one person, on their own. Do you think you can do it? You'll need to start with the mainsail and then move on to the smaller sails."

"Just tell me what to do," said Ben.

"I'll hold the ship steady, while you winch. Here we go. The biggest one first," said the Captain.

Ben struggled to turn the winch, at the bottom of the tallest mast, but the heavy sail refused to move. He pushed harder, but still nothing happened. "I can't shift it. I think it's caught at the top, Sir," he said. At that moment, *The Breeze* listed dangerously, and Ben was nearly swept off his feet. He watched as the card table and several large buckets were swept overboard. The timbers creaked ominously. It felt as though *The Breeze* was being shaken apart.

Ben shivered. "I'll go up and have a look," he said, as he grabbed the rope ladder and began to climb.

"Come down, Ben," called Captain Bluebottle, his

heart in his mouth. "It's too dangerous!"

But Ben took no notice, as he continued to inch his way slowly upwards. He held on to the wildly-swinging ladder for dear life. It took all his strength to climb from one rung to the next, without being blown off. He forgot to be afraid and put all his effort into not falling. Step by slow step, he climbed higher and higher towards the crow's nest.

"Keep safe, Ben," whispered his father, as he watched him disappear into the dark, rainy haze.

"Don't look down! Don't look down!" Ben whispered to himself, as he finally arrived at the top of the mast. With a huge sigh of relief, he pulled himself into the crow's nest and sat for a moment to catch his breath. The rain and the wind stung his eyes. It made it difficult for him to see.

Crash! The mast swung downwards, nearly throwing him sideways into the air. Crash! It swung upwards! Ouch! He was thrown backwards against the side of the cage. It was like being in a washing machine.

Undaunted, he wiped his eyes and held on tight, while he leaned out to get a better look. The heavy sail flapped in the wind, making it hard for him to see where the trouble lay, so he held on with his feet and pulled himself forward. At last, he could see the problem. The sail was snagged on the top of the mast. He grabbed at it, but it was just too far away.

He gripped even tighter with his feet and stretched himself further forward, until he could just reach. He took hold and gave the sail an almighty yank. It came free, leaving him swinging upside down, holding on only by his legs. He waited until the mast swung back the other way, then, very, very carefully, pulled himself back to the safety of the crow's nest. He breathed a huge sigh of relief and started the long climb back down to the deck.

"Thank goodness you're safe." cried Captain Bluebottle, when Ben finally reappeared from the gloom and reached the bottom rung. "Don't you ever do that again! You hear me?"

"Yes, Sir. Whatever you say, Sir," said Ben, as he unwound himself from the rope ladder and rubbed his aching shoulders.

He took hold of the winch and struggled to turn it. One small turn at a time, until slowly, oh so very slowly, the big sail came all the way down. Straight away *The Breeze* seemed to move more happily through the huge waves.

Ben then turned his attention to the smaller sails and in no time at all, they too were down. "All done, Captain," he said, as he secured the last sail. He stood back and looked up, up, up towards the crow's nest. He could see the rope ladder swinging in the wind.

His stomach began to churn. "I – I – think I'm going to be sick," he gasped, as he turned greener than an unripe banana.

"Anything else I can do to help, Captain. Ooooh! Aaaagh! There goes my dinner! I'm not feeling too good at all. What would you like me to do?

"Ooooh! Aaaagh! Here we go again!"

Poor Ben turned greener and greener.

"It's okay, Ben," said Captain Bluebottle gently. "You've done a fine job, but now you need to rest. You go to bed. Roger and I'll take care of *The Breeze*."

All through the night, Captain Bluebottle sailed his ship through huge stormy seas towards the treasure.

There was roaring thunder. There was flashing lightning. There were huge winds, which lifted the ship, pushing her forward at a great speed. There were monstrous waves to climb and steep valleys to surf. Icy lashings of rain made it almost impossible for Captain Bluebottle to see.

Hour after hour the storm raged, becoming wilder and wilder. Hour after hour he held that wheel and steered that ship onwards. Hour after hour the crew stayed below.

"Yikes!" squawked Roger, as he blew backwards from bow to stern.

"Yikes!" squawked Roger as he tumbled once more from the rigging.

"YIKES!"

"This is the best storm I ever had," shouted Captain Bluebottle, as the wind whipped his hair and the rain stung his eyes.

CHAPTER 13

Where Are We?

Some time, just before morning, Captain Bluebottle began to feel the first stirrings of change. The wind didn't feel quite so strong and he could stand without falling over. In a while, all traces of the wild weather had gone, leaving a quiet ocean and the beginnings of a beautiful day. A faint sun began to push its way through the clouds, lighting the ocean with a bright pink sunrise.

"Beautiful, just blooming beautiful," said Captain Bluebottle. "Come on Roger, let's get some breakfast."

But Roger stayed up, perched high on the tallest spar. He was jumping up and down, pointing one wing into the distance and squawking furiously, "Land! Land! **LAND!**"

"What on earth is that parrot talking about now? There's no land around here. Roger, stop mumbling! What are you pointing at?" called Captain Bluebottle. "Hang on, I'll get my telescope."

He took his telescope and pointed it in the direction that Roger was pointing. He couldn't see much at first, just lots of seawater, so he raised his sights and all he could see was a lot of air, so he lowered his sights just a touch ...and there it was! He could just see what looked like an island with a long white beach and three palm trees. He counted them again, just to make sure. One, two, three. Yes, there were three palm trees.

Three palm trees!

He felt a tingle of excitement run right up his spine. He could just about taste the happiness. He could hardly believe his eyes.

"Land! It is land! The best storm ever has blown us to land! And not just any old land. It's Three Palm Island! The best storm has blown us right to the treasure! And not only that... it's got us here a week early! Good spotting, Roger!

"Matey, Cookie, come and help me put up the sails," he called, "There's land just ahead!"

"What's all that noise? Can't a person get a moment's peace and quiet on this ship?" grumbled the First Mate, as he rolled over and went right back to sleep.

"Wake me up when we get there," grumbled the Cook. A moment later, his loud snores could be heard coming from below.

Poor green Ben was still feeling sick. He got up to help, but the cabin was moving too fast. Around and around it went. His head twirled, and his stomach turned somersaults. He crawled back into bed.

"I guess we'll have to do it ourselves, Roger," said Captain Bluebottle. And they did.

It wasn't an easy job for the Captain and his parrot. There were ropes to haul, heavy sails to set and a course to steer. The midday sun was high in the sky when they reached their destination.

"We'll anchor over there, Roger, and we'll row ashore in the morning," said Captain Bluebottle. "Let's wake up our lazy crew. We need to get the sails down quick smart. You and I will have a break and then we'll have dinner. I'm so hungry, I swear I could eat an old gumboot."

"Cookie, Matey, wake up!" he shouted.

Nothing happened. Just the sound of snoring floating up from below.

"Cookie, Matey, wake up now!"

Still nothing.

Captain Bluebottle had finally had enough. He filled a big bucket with extra cold seawater and made his way below decks.

Splosh! He tossed the water over Matey and Cookie. It was cold, it was wet, and it certainly did the job. They woke up and shot out of their bunks, to stand before the Captain with their teeth chattering and their clothes dripping onto the floor.

"What did you do that for, Captain?" they complained.

"I'm tired, Men. It's my turn to sleep and it's your turn to work. The storm has passed and there's a lot of work to be done. You can start by taking the sails down. We're close to an island and I don't want to run ashore."

"But what island?" grumbled the First Mate. "There aren't any islands around here."

"No talking!" ordered the Captain. 'I've written you a list."

1. Take the sails down
2. Scrub the decks and tidy the ship

3. Have a bath
4. Catch fish for dinner
5. Set the table
6. Cook dinner
7. Wake the Captain, Ben and Roger for dinner

"I can help too, Captain. I'm feeling better now," said Ben, sleepily, from the other bunk.

"Go back to sleep, Ben" said Captain Bluebottle. "You did your bit last night. You too, Roger. We all need our rest.

"Any questions, Men?"

The Cook and the First Mate stood there, with their feet in a puddle and their mouths wide open.

"What island?" asked Cookie.

"You'll find out what island when you have finished your jobs," said Captain Bluebottle. "I'm going to my cabin now. Let me know when dinner is ready."

The Captain, Ben and Roger settled down for a well-earned rest, while the First Mate and Cook went on deck to begin their chores.

"I don't see why we have to do everything. Why can't that lazy Cabin Boy help? He's such a spoilt baby," grumbled the First Mate.

"He's not such a bad kid. I quite like him," said Cookie, as he started to winch down the mainsail. "Give me a hand with these sails, Matey. It's too big a job for just one man."

"I still don't know where that flaming island came from," grumbled the First Mate, as the sail came down.

"What's so special about that flaming island anyway?" asked the Cook, as he filled a bucket to scrub the deck.

"Don't just stand there, Matey. These jobs won't get done by themselves. We both need to help."

At last the ship cleaning was done and it was bath time.

"It's only a flaming desert island, with three flaming palm trees!" grumbled Cookie, as he dived into the blue water, holding a large cake of lavender soap.

"Did you say, 'three palm trees', Cookie?" shouted the First Mate, as he bobbed up and down in the water with excitement. "Three flaming palm trees! That's it! Remember the map! The treasure is on Three Palm Island! We're here! Last night's storm must have blown us right to the treasure island! We're here already!"

"Cor, blimey, you might be right," said Cookie. "Come on, Matey. Let's get our jobs finished as quickly as we can. You finish your bath, then give me a hand. We need to be ready to hunt for the treasure tomorrow!"

The First Mate worked hard to catch some fat fish for dinner and to set the table. He even cleaned the fish without complaining, which was something new for him.

Cookie cooked the fish and made a beautiful salad, with sea lettuce and other delicious seafoody stuff. It smelled divine.

The delicious aroma wafted into the Captain's cabin and tickled his nose. "Mmmmmm..." murmured Captain Bluebottle, as he rolled over and sniffed again. "Is that fish and seafoody salad I can smell, Roger? Come on. It's time to get up. You wake Ben and I'll meet you at the dinner table."

"Dinner!" said Roger, as he flew below decks.

"Delicious, Cookie," said Captain Bluebottle, after a very tasty meal. "Here's to Three Palm Island and tomorrow's treasure, Men,"

"To Three Palm Island and tomorrow's treasure!" burped the happy crew.

Captain Bluebottle and his crew talked treasure well into the night. They made plans and carefully gathered essential supplies and provisions.

"Get some rest now, Men, we'll leave after breakfast," he said, when everything was ready.

CHAPTER 14

A Bad Bunch of Stinky Pirates

Meanwhile, on the other side of the island, there was another party going on. This wasn't just any old party. This was a pirate party! This was the private pirate party of Captain Marmaduke Mustard and his swashbuckling crew.

And what an ugly bunch they were...

There was the boss pirate, Captain Marmaduke Mustard, the meanest pirate on the seven seas. He had a bushy beard with wriggly things living in it. He had a big pimply nose and fat, lardy cheeks. When he smiled, which wasn't often, you could see a big gold filling surrounded by dirty teeth. He had mean, squinty, little eyes, which never stopped moving.

His shirt did up over his belly with a row of pure gold buttons. His pants were studded with real pearls and his boots were buckled with real diamond studs. Captain Marmaduke Mustard loved treasure a lot.

"Here's to the treasure," he hiccoughed, showing his gold filling, as he gulped down another slug of rum. "Here's to next week when Captain Bluebottle arrives." Gulp! "Here's to next week when my brother, Brian, arrives." Gulp! "Here's to next week when we steal the treasure from Captain Bluebottle and his crew. And here's to piracy, swearing and bad manners." Hiccough!

"Here's to the treasure," gulped Mr. Sly, the second in command, as he chewed a large piece of fish pie, while at the same time, he picked his nose. He was a very grubby pirate, with no manners at all. His idea of a good time was to bully the rest of the crew mercilessly. He carried a cruel cat 'o nine tails whip, shoved into his belt, which he would bring out whenever he got grumpy ... which was often. The only part of his body that worked well was his big mouth. He belched and threw the remains of the pie into the sea. "This pie is putrid! Get some decent food up here right away, Cook! I'm hungry!"

"What?" asked the Pirate Cook, from a large

hammock, strung between the two masts. He opened his eyes and scratched a large pimple on his chin. "You want me, the Chef, to fetch more food? I don't fetch food, I cook it. Get the boy to fetch it!" His double chins wobbled indignantly. Having got that off his chest, he rolled over and settled back down into the hammock.

"Cabin Boy! Get me another rum! And be quick about it!" shouted Captain Mustard to Pete, the Cabin Boy.

"I'm being as quick as I can, Captain Mustard, Sir," stuttered Pete. He took the bottle and poured a large rum. As he did so some of it spilt out of the mug and trickled down the Captain's sleeve. Pete willed him not to notice. "Here's your rum, Sir. Will there be anything else, Sir?"

"Yes, get out of my sight, Boy!" shouted the Pirate Captain.

It was hard to tell how old Pete was. He was such an insignificant looking little person. He was pale, skinny and his clothes didn't fit. His idea of a good time was to eat a plate of good food. He usually only got leftovers and scraps.

"Go below and bring up some decent food for Captain Mustard and me," ordered Mr. Sly.

"Yes, Mr. Sly, Sir," stuttered Pete. He rushed down the gangway to the galley below. He ran so fast that he skidded on the greasy floor, lost his balance and came to rest against the leg of a grubby table. That really hurt! Tears came to his eyes, but he wiped them away and pulled himself to his feet.

He looked around.

As far as ship's galleys go, this was truly disgusting. The floor was filthy, and all the benches were covered with smelly old stuff...like seven-day old beans, slimy eggshells, fish bones, crumbs of old toast and rancid milk. There was a smell about it, hard to describe, but unimaginably bad. Flies and cockroaches scurried backwards and forwards through the muck.

With his stomach heaving, Pete piled a plate with unappetizing-looking food and hobbled nervously back up to the deck. Captain Mustard and Mr. Sly were deep in conversation. "This is all the food I could find, Sir," he said. He put the plate on the table and stood back, just avoiding a swipe from Mr. Sly's cat 'o nine tails.

"I told you not to interrupt me, when I'm speaking, Boy. Now get out of my sight!"

"Yes, Sir," said Pete, gratefully, as he took off to safety.

"What's the plan, Captain Mustard?" asked Mr. Sly. "Do we attack Captain Bluebottle and his crew as soon as they arrive next week? Or do we wait until they reach the beach? I think we should hit them as soon as they arrive. We'll jump their ship when it drops anchor, we'll tie up the crew and steal the treasure map. Then we'll go and get the treasure for ourselves! That's how we'll do it, Captain."

"Are you daft, Sly?" asked Captain Mustard. "That's the silliest plan I've ever heard. Listen up, this is how we'll do it...

"...We'll wait. We'll wait, and we'll watch. We'll wait until they have found the treasure. We'll wait until they have dug up the treasure. We'll wait until they have carried the treasure all the way back to the beach. Then we'll strike. That way they'll do all the hard work and we'll get the reward. It'll be so easy! They'll be too tired to fight back. We'll get the treasure and then we'll take their ship! That's a very good plan."

"And the parrot, Captain," mumbled Cook, as he opened one eye, and licked his lips. "We'll get the treasure, the ship and the parrot. I have an excellent recipe for parrot pie, Captain. Crusty parrot pie with a pastry topping. Mmmmmm! The thought of it is making my lips tingle! You can't beat it," he burped, as he closed his eyes again.

"You'll have your parrot, Cook," said the pirate boss, with a cruel smirk. "You'll have your parrot and I'll have my treasure and the ship. Get me another rum, Boy, I feel like celebrating tonight."

CHAPTER 15

Three Palm Island

The next morning Captain Bluebottle and the crew of *The Breeze* woke early, keen to get on their way. They packed the rowboat with spades and shovels, a compass, water bottles, several large sacks, sandwiches, Captain Bluebottle's blunderbuss (for fighting pirates) and, of course, the treasure map. At last they were ready.

"Let's go, Crew," shouted Captain Bluebottle. "Let's go and get the treasure! Keep your eyes open for pirates, Men. You never know where they might be lurking!"

"Aye, aye, Captain!" shouted Ben and Cook, as they started to row.

"Pirates!" squawked Roger, as he sat on Captain Bluebottle's shoulder and looked important.

"Yes, Sir, Captain, Sir, I'll keep my eyes open all the way," said the First Mate. "I'll keep watch while you men row. Yes, Sir, we don't want any nasty pirates stealing our treasure."

"That's the way, Matey," said Captain Bluebottle, as he steered the small boat towards Three Palm Island.

Before too long they arrived at a beautiful sandy

beach. They pulled the boat out of the water and dragged it up onto the shore, past the high tide line.

Captain Bluebottle unfolded the treasure map and looked around. "Let's see. There are three palm trees just like the map. There's a rocky headland over there on the right and a mountain over there. This is looking good. Ben, can you have a look over that ridge and see if you can find a river? Keep an eye out for crocodiles and pirates!"

"Aye, aye, Captain!" shouted Ben, as he disappeared over the ridge.

CHAPTER 16

No More Fishcakes!

Meanwhile, back at the pirate ship, the smelly pirates were all on deck, doing what pirates do best...grumbling.

"What sort of food do you call this?" screamed Captain Mustard, as he tipped a plate of stinky fish cakes over the Cook's head. "I'm sick of fish! We've had fish every day for the past month. I want something new for lunch! Something sweet! So, get me something sweet for lunch or you'll walk the plank!"

"You heard the Captain," echoed Mr. Sly. "Some decent food, Cook! Or it's the plank for you!"

"What do they think I am?" grumbled Cook, under his breath. A flaming magician or something? Where am I supposed to get something sweet? There's only flaming fish to cook! Aaaaaagh!"

"Excuse me, Cook, Sir," whispered Pete. "What about a coconut cream pie for lunch? There are three palm trees on the other side of the island. I could get a couple of coconuts for you if you like."

"Well, what are you still standing there for, Boy?" yelled the ungrateful cook. "Go and get some coconuts! And don't come back until you've got them!"

"Yes, Sir," Pete took off like a startled rabbit, heading straight for the other side of the island and the three palm trees.

"I've just had an excellent idea, Captain," said Cook, in his slimiest voice. "I've decided to cook you a coconut cream pie for lunch. I'm just waiting on the coconuts."

"That's better, Cook," said Captain Mustard. "If it tastes sweet and delicious, I might just let you off the plank walking. We'll see..."

It wasn't easy to get to the other side of the island. It was a long way; along sandy beaches, through muddy bogs, around rugged rocks and over high cliffs. Pete trudged on, afraid to stop. What if there were snakes or wild animals. He didn't want to think about it. He shivered and walked faster. Two hours later, he rounded the headland, only to see Captain Bluebottle, First Mate and Cook in the distance. They were so busy studying the treasure map that they didn't notice him, as he scurried behind some rocks for cover.

"Uh oh, they're early," mumbled Pete, his teeth chattering. "They've come early! I need to tell Captain Mustard. Ooooh, he's going to be so angry!"

With that he took off back to the pirate ship as fast as his tired legs would carry him.

CHAPTER 17

Buried Treasure!

"I've found a river, Captain." Ben puffed, as he reappeared over the ridge. "It's not too far from here. It's just down the slope on the other side. I didn't see any pirates or crocodiles."

"Perfect," said Captain Bluebottle. He looked up from the treasure map. "This is so exciting, Men. Look here... just like the map ... there's the three palms, there's the mountain in the distance, the rocky headland and the river. This is our Treasure Island! No doubt about it!

"Now let's see, we need to start by the tallest palm, line up with the top of the mountain and go over the ridge to the river. Come on, Men, follow me! Let's go and get us some treasure."

"Aye, aye, Captain," said Ben and Cookie.

"Lead the way, Captain. Cookie and Ben, you carry the supplies and I'll keep watch for any pirates," said the First Mate. He picked up the blunderbuss and following behind.

The crew started at the tallest palm and made a beeline for the mountain. They went over the ridge at a fast pace and in no time at all they arrived at the river. It was a peaceful picture. Pretty flowers covered the banks and brightly colored butterflies filled the air. There were even red and green parrots perched in the trees, chattering away to each other.

Captain Bluebottle waded into the river. He had only gone a few steps when the water reached up to his chest. "It's too deep to walk across," he said, as he turned for the shore. "We need to get ourselves and our supplies across to the other side somehow. Any ideas, Men?"

"It doesn't look too wide, Captain," said Ben, as he tied a rope around his waist. "I could probably swim this rope over to the other side, then pull you all over?"

"That would be great, Ben. Keep an eye out for crocodiles and other nasty stuff," called the Captain, as Ben dived in.

Ben didn't need to be told to swim quickly...he cut through the water like a torpedo. There was no way that he was going to get caught by a crocodile, a piranha, a blood-sucking leech, or anything else nasty. In no time at all he hauled himself out on to the other bank, tied the rope to a sturdy tree and swam back to help carry the supplies.

Brian kept watch, while Captain Bluebottle, Cook and Ben made several trips across the river, each holding the safety rope with one hand, whilst holding the supplies above their heads, with the other. Meanwhile Roger flew from tree to tree, chattering with the colorful birds. The air was filled with the sound of them all talking together.

"Good job, Ben," said Captain Bluebottle, as he reached the other side for the final time and lowered his heavy load to the ground. "That's everything. Now let's see, where do we go from here?"

The crew sat under the tree to gather their breath, as they checked the map.

"The map shows that we must turn towards the north-north-west and walk across Snake Gully until we reach Overhang Rock. I don't like the sound of that much. We'd better stick together and keep an eye out for snakes. And pirates! Keep that blunderbuss at the ready, Matey."

"Maybe I should wait here and keep watch until you come back, Captain," suggested the Brian. "That way, I'll be able to stop any pirates before they cross the river."

"No, I think we'd all better stay together, Matey. It would be much too dangerous for you to stay on your own. We'll all stick together and keep safe," said Captain Bluebottle. He took out his compass and pointed ahead. "North-north-west, that's the way. Let's go, Men, I can feel that treasure getting closer and closer. Come on, Roger. It's time to go."

Ben gulped, as he lifted his share of the load onto his shoulders. "Stay close to me, Cookie," he whispered. "I'm scared of snakes!"

"Me too," whispered Cookie. "But I did hear that they taste quite nice, fried with a little butter. Maybe we could get Brian to catch us a nice snake or two for dinner. What do you think?"

Ben giggled. "The only thing Brian's good at catching is new ways to get out of work," he whispered.

"Keep up you two!" called Brian, as he strode after Captain Bluebottle, carrying just the blunderbuss.

Snake Gulch turned out to be a dry, dusty canyon between high cliffs. Sharp rocks made the going tough and prickly thistles grabbed at the crew as they went past. And, then there were the snakes... lots and lots of snakes. Small ones, big ones, fat ones, thin ones, of many different colors and patterns.

"Stamp your feet as you walk!" ordered Captain Bluebottle. "These snakes are much more afraid of us than we are of them."

"You're right," said Ben, stamping his foot. A red and white striped snake shot out from under a rock and headed for safety. He stamped his foot again. "How much further, Captain? We seem to be coming to the end of the trail."

"Not much further now. That looks like Overhang Rock up ahead. We'll stop there, take a break and check the map."

At last they reached the enormous rock. It towered over them and cast its huge shadow across the dry earth. They eased the supplies off their aching shoulders and took a well-earned rest in the shade.

"Okay," said the Captain, as he checked the map. "We're here at Overhang Rock and according to this, we're not too far away from the treasure now. We just need to head north-east for five hundred and twenty-three paces." He took out his compass and lined up the north-east. "That's in this direction. Are you ready, Men? Here we go again. Don't forget to count.

"One, two, three...Here we go, past this big rock...

"...one hundred and twenty-five, one hundred and twenty-six... Keep counting, Men. We don't want to have to start again...

"...three hundred and eighty-six, three hundred and eighty-seven, three hundred and eighty-eight... Just let me check the compass again.

"North-east. Yes, that's right...

"...four hundred and two... four hundred and three... Not far to go now, we're nearly there...

"...five hundred and twenty-one, five hundred and twenty-two, five
hundred and twenty-three!

"We've arrived! According to the map, we're here. This looks like the right place. Now, the map says that X marks the spot. We just need to find the X."

The tired crew looked around. They were in a small clearing, surrounded by tall trees. Captain Bluebottle, Ben and Cookie set about looking for the X, while Brian sat on a large rock in the middle of the clearing and did nothing to help. They searched everywhere, but couldn't find an X anywhere.

"Don't give up, Men," said the Captain. "It's got to be here somewhere. Check everywhere again.

"Brian, we all need to help. We're not going to find it by sitting around."

Ben watched, as Brian reluctantly stood up. His attention was immediately drawn to a large X, carved into the rock, which Brian had been sitting on. "There it is! The X! Brian's been sitting on it! It was underneath him all the time!" he shouted.

"All the time!" squawked Roger.

The First Mate glared.

"You're right, Ben," said the Captain. "X marks the spot! That's where we'll dig for the treasure!"

"Splendid, Captain," said the First Mate. "I'll keep a lookout for pirates while you all dig." He stomped off into the trees, to find a shady place to sit.
Captain Bluebottle, Cookie and Ben lifted the rock and took turns digging for what seemed like hours. They

sweated in the tropical heat, but they didn't give up. Just when they were beginning to think that there was no treasure after all, Ben's spade hit something solid. Clunk! He dug faster. Clunk! There it was again! "Captain, there's something here," he shouted.

Captain Bluebottle and Cookie hopped into the large hole to help and in no time at all they uncovered an ornate, wooden chest. It was very heavy, and it took quite a lot of team work and puffing and panting to lift it, but they managed it.

At last the chest was out of the hole and the three workers put down their shovels for a well-earned rest. Brian was still nowhere to be seen. He was sitting on a rock just around the corner, watching for pirates.

"Good work, Men," gasped Captain Bluebottle. "I think we need to take a break now, I'm almost too tired to be excited." No one noticed him pick up an ornate key from the bottom of the hole and slip it into his pocket. "We'll have some lunch and then we'll carry the treasure back to the ship."

"Lunchtime, Matey," he shouted.

Upon hearing the word 'lunchtime', First Mate very quickly took time out from his pirate-watching duties. "Let's open the chest now, Captain," he said, as he chewed on a shrimp sandwich. "Let's see what's inside this beauty." He started to pull at the lid, but it wouldn't budge.

He pulled again. Nothing happened. He tried to wedge the shovel under the lock, but it held fast. He tried to bash it open with a heavy rock, but the rock bounced off and hit him on the chin. He sat down with a snarl and glared at the treasure chest.

"Don't worry, Matey," said Captain Bluebottle. "We'll find a way to open it when we get back to the ship. Have another sandwich."

After a short rest, the Captain and his hardworking crew were ready to start the journey back to the ship. "I'll go ahead and look out for pirates," offered the First Mate, as he picked up the blunderbuss and led the way.

Captain Bluebottle, Cook and Ben hoisted the heavy chest onto their shoulders and set out. It was hard work. Sometimes they stumbled and almost fell. The First Mate strolled ahead looking for pirates.

It took a long, long time, but at last the exhausted chest-carriers arrived back at the ridge near the shore. "Not far to go now," gasped Captain Bluebottle. He climbed to the top of the ridge and looked towards the shore. The beach was deserted, and it looked peaceful, but there was a very unpleasant smell wafting in on the breeze.

"Yuk! What's that disgusting smell!" gasped Cookie. He retched and covered his nose with his hand. "It's putrid!"

It was putrid all right!

"Ugh! It smells like whale fart!" gasped Ben. "It seems to be coming from that direction and it's getting stronger."

"I know that smell well," said Captain Bluebottle. "That's not whale fart. That's pirate. That's what it is. That's the stink of particularly bad pirates. We need to get out of sight right now, Men. Move back. Get the treasure out of sight. That's it. Keep your heads down! Quickly now!"

The Captain and his crew wriggled back down the ridge to safety.

Brian stood up. He hoisted the blunderbuss onto his shoulder and puffed out his chest. "Let me check it out, Captain," he said. "I'll sneak up and have a look. I'll find out what they're up to, then I'll come back and let you know what's going on."

"Stay safe, Matey," said Captain Bluebottle.

"Don't worry, Captain," said the First Mate. He patted the blunderbuss. "This will keep me safe. I'll fill those pirates with buckshot if they come too close." He moved silently over the ridge and in a moment was gone.

"He's a brave man, that Matey," said Captain Bluebottle, as he took the key out of his pocket. "Hand me those sacks, Ben. We've work to do, and we haven't got much time."

CHAPTER 18

A Very Sneaky Plan

Meanwhile Brian, the First Mate, followed the stinky smell to the rocky headland. He felt very excited.

"Hey, Bro!" he called softly. "Where are you? I can smell you, but I can't see you." He picked his way among the rocks. He looked everywhere but saw no pirates.

Suddenly, in the distance, he spied something coming quickly towards him. As it got closer, he could see that it wasn't one thing ... it was four things. It was four bodies! It was the Pirate Chief and his crew. Coming fast! As they got closer, the foul smell became even stronger.

"Why are you early, Brian?" puffed Captain Mustard, as he staggered up. "You told me that you wouldn't be here for a week! You've messed up all my plans. Now I have no idea how we're going to get the treasure! I should box your ears!"

"Nice to see you too, Bro," said the First Mate. "Calm down and listen. I have a plan.

"They've already found the treasure and we can take it from them in the blink of an eye. Captain Bluebottle thinks that I'm on his side. The silly old fool sent me here to check on you, for goodness sake! We'll have that treasure come to us, without having to move a muscle. This is what we'll do.

"We'll send the Cabin Boy back with a message to say that I've been captured by pirates and that they'll chop off my head if he doesn't bring the treasure here immediately. He'll come to save me, for sure. He's like that... a bit weak in the head.

"When he comes we'll grab him, his pesky crew, his ship and the treasure and we'll tie them to those three palm trees over there and that will be the end of that. What do you think, Bro?"

"Hmmm. It is a good plan, Brian," said Captain Mustard. "It should work a treat. You heard the man, Pete. Get out there and give that Bluebottle my message. The rest of us will hide behind these rocks until they come. And then we'll grab them!"

"Aye, aye Captain, Sir" said Pete. "I'm on my way, Sir."

"Just shut up and go," roared Captain Mustard.

CHAPTER 19

Captured!

"That should do it," said Captain Bluebottle, as he relocked the treasure chest. "Ben, would you mind looking to see if there is any sign of Matey coming back. He's been away a long time."

"Aye, aye, Captain," said Ben, as he crawled to the top of the ridge for a better look.

Slowly he inched his way to the top and peeked over. "There's someone coming, and it's not Matey!" he shouted. "Look out, he's coming our way!"

He jumped up and tackled Pete. He pushed him roughly to the ground and sat on him.

"Ow! Get off me!" wailed Pete. He wriggled this way and that, as he tried to escape. But Ben just sat tight and held him captive.

"What on earth are you?" asked Captain Bluebottle, as he bent down to look at this smelly creature. "Are you a boy, or are you a pirate? You don't look old enough to be a pirate. What are you?"

Pete sniffed, "I'm just Pete, Sir. I was a boy once, Sir...I really was. Then, one day, Captain Mustard stole me away from my home and took me to sea. I haven't seen my Mum or Dad since. It's been so long. Now I don't know who I am." A big tear rolled down his cheek and he wiped it away with a dirty sleeve. "Please don't hurt me!"

"That's horrible," said Ben. "No one's going to hurt you." He helped Pete to his feet and put an arm around his skinny shoulders.

"Captain Mustard made me come with a message for you," whispered Pete. "He said to tell you that he's captured your First Mate and that he will chop off his head if you don't bring the treasure to him right away. I've got to go back now. If I don't go back straight away, he'll beat me. Please, Sir, let me go."

"Of course, you can go, Pete," said Captain Bluebottle. "Tell that nasty Pirate Chief that I'm on my way, with the treasure chest. And try not to worry. Everything will be all right."

Pete scampered back across the sand towards the rocks.

Captain Bluebottle lifted one end of the chest and sighed. "Come on, Men, let's get this over and done with," he said. "Hurry! Poor Matey is in trouble."

With heavy hearts, they carried the chest over the ridge and down to the beach. When they reached the rocks, they stopped and looked around nervously. There was no sign of the pirates. "What do you think they will do to us?" whispered Ben.

Captain Bluebottle had no time to reply.

At that moment the pirate chief leapt up from behind the rocks, with a bloodcurdling scream. He was a terrifying sight as he waved his cutlass and shouted, "Stop there, Bluebottle! Stop right there, all of you, and put your hands up! You are my prisoners!"

"Yes, stop there!" came another voice, from behind the rocks...a quite familiar voice. "Stop there, Captain

Bluebottle!"

"Matey, is that you?" called Captain Bluebottle. "Are you all right? Have the pirates hurt you? Don't worry, we've brought the treasure to save you."

The First Mate's head popped up. "Yes, it's me, Brian, and I'm just fine! I fooled you all! I'm not a First Mate, I'm a pirate and this is my brother, Captain Marmaduke Mustard, the big boss of all the seas. He's in charge now, so make sure that you all do as you're told." He giggled a disgusting giggle and looked most ferocious.

"Tie them all up to those palm trees over there, Pete," ordered Captain Mustard. "Tie them up tight, or I'll box your ears. I'll figure out what to do with them in the morning."

"Yes, Sir," said Pete.

He tied Captain Bluebottle, Cookie and Ben to the palm trees, with lots of rope. "Sorry, Sir," he whispered to the Captain, as he tied the last knot.

"It's not your fault, Pete," whispered Ben.

"Keep quiet, Prisoners," ordered the pirate chief. "Brian and Sly, you get the parrot. Cook's going to make us a delicious parrot pie for dinner. It'll be a change from fish this and fish that. I can't wait." He licked his lips.

"Help!" squawked Roger, as he flew to the top of the highest palm to hide among the leaves.

"Aye, aye, Bro," said Brian, as he picked up the blunderbuss. "Stand back, Sly, I'm going to pepper that pesky parrot with buckshot. Be ready to catch him, when he drops."

Mr. Sly stood under the palm tree, with his arms open, as Brian lined up his sights and took aim.

BOOM went the blunderbuss and a shower of coconut fronds floated down to the ground.

"Missed!" squawked Roger, as he flew sideways to the next tree.

Brian lined up his sights again. "Stand still, Bird," he ordered. BOOM went the blunderbuss again. More fronds. No parrot.

"Missed!" squawked Roger again.

Ben felt a laugh coming on. He tried hard to hold it in, but it just popped out. He couldn't help it. He laughed and laughed, until tears ran down his cheeks.

As if Brian wasn't angry enough already! This made him even angrier. His face went all red and he looked like he was ready to explode.

"You think it's funny, do you, little Cabin Boy?" he roared. "I'll show you what's funny. Funny is a taste of Mr. Sly's whip, around your legs. That's what's funny! Give me your cat o' nine tails, Sly. I've been waiting for this moment for a long time." He took off his hat, rolled up his sleeves and spat on his hands.

Ben shivered. He waited bravely for the first lash.

High in the coconut palm, Roger positioned himself.

"I'll teach you manners, Boy," said Brian, as he raised the cruel whip over his shoulder.

SPLAT! A big blob of parrot poo splattered on to his head.

"Bullseye," shouted Ben.

"Bullseye!" squawked Roger, as he lined up for another barrage.

"Yuk! Get that disgusting bird away from me!" screamed Brian, as he dived into the sea, to wash the gooey mess from his hair.

Head cleaned and clothes dripping, he stomped back up the beach towards the palm trees. "I'll get you and I'll get your filthy parrot, Boy! Just you wait!" He waved the whip at Ben. As he got nearer, Roger lined up again.

Brian backed off, in a real temper.

Captain Mustard chuckled, "This is better than the movies. Forget the bird for a moment, Boys," he said. "We'll sneak up on him later when he's not looking. And don't worry about the Cabin Boy, Captain Smartypants or the Cook. Tomorrow you can be in charge when they walk the plank."

"Thanks, Bro," said Brian. "I can't wait!"

"Cook, you light the fire. We'll camp here overnight, and our prisoners will carry the treasure to the ship in the morning," ordered the Pirate Captain.

"Aye, aye, Captain," said the Cook, as he hurried to follow orders.

"Pete, you sit there and watch the prisoners. If they move or talk, let me know."

"Yes, Sir," said Pete.

"Brian and Sly, give me a hand to get this treasure chest open. Let's find out what booty Captain Smartypants and his crew have brought us. If you both hold it tight, I should be able to prise it open."

Captain Mustard tried to force open the treasure chest with his cutlass, but he had no luck. He tried it from every angle, but the lid wouldn't budge.

He threw down his cutlass with disgust and kicked the chest. Ow! That made his toe hurt! "We'll open the flaming chest when we get back to the ship tomorrow," he said, as he took off his boot and rubbed his sore foot.

Brian and Mr. Sly took random pot shots at Roger

throughout the afternoon, but they missed every time. They became angrier and angrier as the afternoon wore on.

Roger squawked, 'Missed again!' from the top of the tallest palm.

"I'll get that flaming parrot if it's the last thing I do!" yelled Brian. He stamped his feet and kicked a flurry of sand into the Pirate Cook's newly-lit fire.

The fire went out.

Cook exploded, "I just got that flaming fire lit and now you've put it out! I give up! If you want anything to eat you can cook it yourself!" He sat down and refused to move. "I'm on strike!" he said.

"Where's that Cabin Boy? What are you doing just sitting around?" shouted Captain Mustard. "Get me a rum, you lazy little lump! Hop to it...NOW!"

"Me too," chorused Brian and Mr. Sly. "Hop to it, Boy!"

"Did someone say 'rum'?" asked Cook.

"Yes, Sirs, I'm hopping," said Pete.

That set the scene for the rest of the afternoon. Four foul-smelling pirates drinking rum, swearing and burping and not getting any happier; three trussed-up prisoners, whispering to each other and trying to look scared; one cheeky parrot calling insults from the treetops and Pete, who was kept busy, pouring more and more rum.

As the afternoon wore on and the shadows began to lengthen, the eyes of the pirates began to get blurry and their speech became muddled. The rum was beginning to work.

"Get me another boy, you lazy rum!" burped Captain Mustard.

"Coming right up, Captain, Sir," said Pete.

As night fell, the bossy voices gradually stopped and soon the sound of pirate snores filled the air.

CHAPTER 20

In the Middle of the Night

In the dark, Ben sat nervously, tied to the palm tree and listened. The sound of the snoring pirates reached his ears. It was time.

"Roger," he whispered. "Where are you?"

A rustle of wings brushed past his ear and he felt a small peck on his hand.

"Squawk," whispered Roger.

"Good Bird," whispered Ben. "See if you can chew through this rope." He felt his friend pulling, with his sharp beak. "Ouch! Just the rope, Roger! Not me! That's better."

In no time at all Roger had chewed through his bonds, setting him free. Ben rubbed his wrists and ankles.

"Great job, Roger," Captain Bluebottle whispered from the next palm tree. "Can you free Cookie, while Ben unties me?"

"Squawk," whispered Roger, and he started chewing again.

"Hold still, Sir," whispered Ben, as he made short work of the Captain's ropes.

"Well done, you two," whispered Captain Bluebottle, as he was freed. He stood up and helped Cookie to his feet. "Quietly now, Men. Let's get the treasure onto the ship and then we can go."

Just then, he felt a hand on his arm, holding him back. It was Ben, with a finger to his lips. He was pointing at something on the beach.

Something moved.

They watched as a ghostly figure rose from the sand and started to move towards them. They froze, hardly daring to breathe.

"We've been found out. It's one of the pirates!" whispered the Captain. "There's only one thing for it. You two jump on him and I'll tie him up. Don't let him make a noise, or he'll tell the others and we'll never escape."

The shadowy form came closer and closer, until it was almost upon them.

"Now!" whispered the Captain.

Ben and Cookie leapt up, grabbed the pirate and pushed him to the ground. Cookie sat on him, while Ben held his hand over his mouth. The pirate wriggled but couldn't escape. He was well and truly caught.

"We'll have to gag him and tie him to a palm tree," said Captain Bluebottle. "Hand me that rope, please, Roger."

"Squawk," whispered Roger.

"Wait!" said Ben. He felt something drip onto his hand. "I think this pirate is crying, Sir," he whispered. "And he feels really skinny. I think it might be Pete."

He took his hand away from the pirate's mouth. "Is that you, Pete?" he whispered.

"Yes, it's me," sniffed Pete, as he wiped a tear from his eye. "Can I come with you? I promise I won't be any trouble. I just want to go back home."

"Of course, you can come," said Captain Bluebottle. 'We'll take you home and we'll find your Mum and Dad. Now, let's get the treasure and get out of here."

"I'll help carry," whispered Pete. He strained to lift a corner of the treasure chest. He looked up in surprise when he saw the others heading over the ridge, soon to reappear, each carrying a big sack.

"Come on, Men, let's get these sacks into the rowboat and out to the ship," whispered Captain Bluebottle. Quietly now, we don't want them to wake up. Come on, Pete. Let's go. Oh, and can you grab some of those coconuts there? We'll take those with us."

"But, Captain. What about the treasure?" asked Pete.

"Don't worry, Pete," whispered Captain Bluebottle, with a wink. "You'll see. Let's go."

Silently they dragged the rowboat into the water,

loaded it with the heavy sacks and rowed out to *The Breeze.* They hauled the sacks on to the deck. Ever so quietly, they raised the sails and the ship slipped out to sea, away from Three Palm Island.

"But, Captain, what about the treasure?" asked Pete. "We didn't get the treasure."

"Well, sit down here, Pete, and I'll tell you all about that," said Captain Bluebottle happily.

CHAPTER 21

The Pirates' Treasure

There wasn't much happiness on the beach at
Three Palm Island the next morning, when the pirates
woke up.

Captain Mustard woke first. He was in a foul mood.
"Get me some breakfast, Cabin Boy!" he ordered, as he
opened his eyes and burped loudly.

Nothing happened.

He tried again. "Hurry up, Boy, or I'll box your
ears!" he shouted.

Nothing happened.

He leapt to his feet and chopped at the air with his
cutlass. ""Brian, Sly, Cook, help me find that boy.
Don't just stand there! Find him! Where is that little
brat!"

But the Pirate Cook didn't move. He stood, with his
mouth wide open, pointing at the palm trees. "C-c-c-
captain," he mumbled. "They've gone! All gone! I think
they've escaped! Look!" He pointed towards the beach.

There were no prisoners tied to the coconut palms
and there was no noisy parrot patrolling above. All that
was left were four sets of footprints in the sand and the
drag line of a rowboat, leading into the sea. Captain

Mustard ran to the shore and looked out.

It was a beautiful day. The sea sparkled in the morning sunlight. The waves washed in and the waves washed out, but there was no ship in sight.

"You let them escape! You flamin' well let them escape and they've taken that brat of a cabin boy with them! Just wait until I get my hands on you!" he shouted. He waved his cutlass in the air and rounded on his terrified crew.

"But Captain, Sir," said Mr. Sly. "They didn't take our treasure! Look! It's still here! All we need to do now is to carry it back to our ship."

There on the sand, was the treasure chest.

"You're right, Sly," said the Captain. "Luckily for you, they left my treasure behind. It was probably too heavy for that Captain Bluebottle, to carry. I always knew he was a weakling! All you need to do now is to carry it back to the ship.

"So, hop to it, Men! Lift that chest and let's get going. I can't wait to get that treasure aboard. Well, what are you waiting for?"

"Aye, aye, Captain," muttered Mr. Sly and Cook, as they lifted the heavy chest onto their shoulders and set off.

"What are you waiting for, Brian?" asked Captain Mustard.

"I thought I'd just keep an eye out for danger," said Brian. "You never know when there might be some danger. I'll just walk behind with my blunderbuss and keep us safe."

"Have you gone bananas, Brian?" said Captain Mustard. "Did a coconut fall on your head while you were asleep and muddle your brain? What have I, the meanest pirate in the whole, wide world, to be afraid of? 'Danger', you say. Huh! The only danger is what will happen to you if you don't help carry that chest! So, hop to it, Brian. What are you waiting for? Now!"

As Brian hurried to help, Captain Mustard followed behind, shouting instructions to his unfortunate crew, as they wrestled with the chest.

It wasn't easy. The chest was heavy, and the day was hot. The pirate crew struggled to keep going in the heat. They stumbled over rough ground, they dragged themselves up steep slopes and they staggered along deserted beaches, until, at last, in the late afternoon, they reached the bay where the pirate ship was anchored.

"I don't think I can go any further," gasped the Cook. He fell to his knees. "Can't we take a break, Captain?"

"Not so soon, Cook. You can take a break when we get there and not before! You need to put the treasure into the dinghy and row it out to the ship. Well, what are you waiting for! Hop to it! Now!" shouted Captain Mustard.

"Aye, aye, Captain," grumbled the exhausted crew, as they loaded the heavy chest onto the small boat.

Mr. Sly and Cook rowed, while Brian steered. Captain Mustard sat in the stern. He was beginning to feel quite excited. "It won't be long now, Men," he said, with a grin.

After lots of puffing and panting, the tired crew reached the ship and hauled the chest on to the deck.

"Bring me my pirate's tool kit," ordered the Captain. "I'm going to take this sucker apart."

"Coming right up, Captain, Sir," said Mr. Sly.

"Stand back, Men, while I give this give this booty box a bash with my biggest hammer," ordered Captain Mustard. He flexed his muscles and lined up the hammer.

Bang! Thump! Crash! The chest shuddered as the Captain attacked it from every angle. Slivers of wood began to fly into the air, as he pounded the hinges. The chest began to shake, and the hinges split.

The excited crew crowded closer in anticipation.

"Stand back, Men!" shouted the Captain. "One last bash should do it."

Crash! The heavy chest fell apart, revealing... heaps and heaps and heaps of river rocks!

CHAPTER 22

Homeward Bound

Meanwhile, *The Breeze* sailed peacefully across the deep, blue ocean. Captain Bluebottle looked at his tired crew. It had been a good day...

First there had been the sacks of treasure. Heaps and heaps and heaps of glorious treasure. There was plenty for everyone. Even Pete.

Then there had been the ship cleaning, with everyone mucking in to help. This had been followed by the crew bathing. Pete certainly smelt a lot better after that.

The perfect day had finished with a scrumptious coconut cream pie, lovingly baked by Cookie and served on real gold plates.

Ben rubbed his full stomach and groaned happily, "This is totally the best adventure I've ever had, Dad. Can we do it again?" he asked.

"Sure, we can," said Captain Bluebottle. He gave Ben a big hug. "But, right now, let's go home, Son."

Made in the USA
Middletown, DE
07 November 2019